The Princess
and the
Christmas Rescue

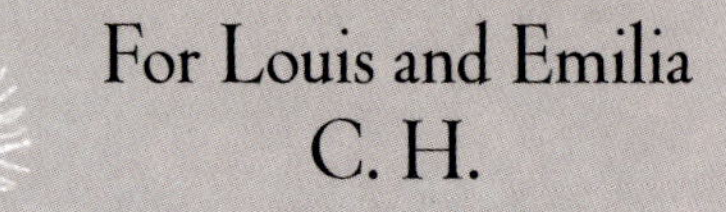

For Louis and Emilia
C. H.

For Dad, who would no doubt find fault in the engineering
S. W.

First U.S. edition 2017

Library of Congress Catalog Card Number pending
ISBN 978-0-7636-9632-0

17 18 19 20 21 22 FGF 10 9 8 7 6 5 4 3 2 1

Printed in Shenzhen, Guangdong, China

This book was typeset in ThrohandInk.
The illustrations were done in mixed media.

Nosy Crow
an imprint of
Candlewick Press
99 Dover Street
Somerville, Massachusetts 02144

www.nosycrow.com
www.candlewick.com

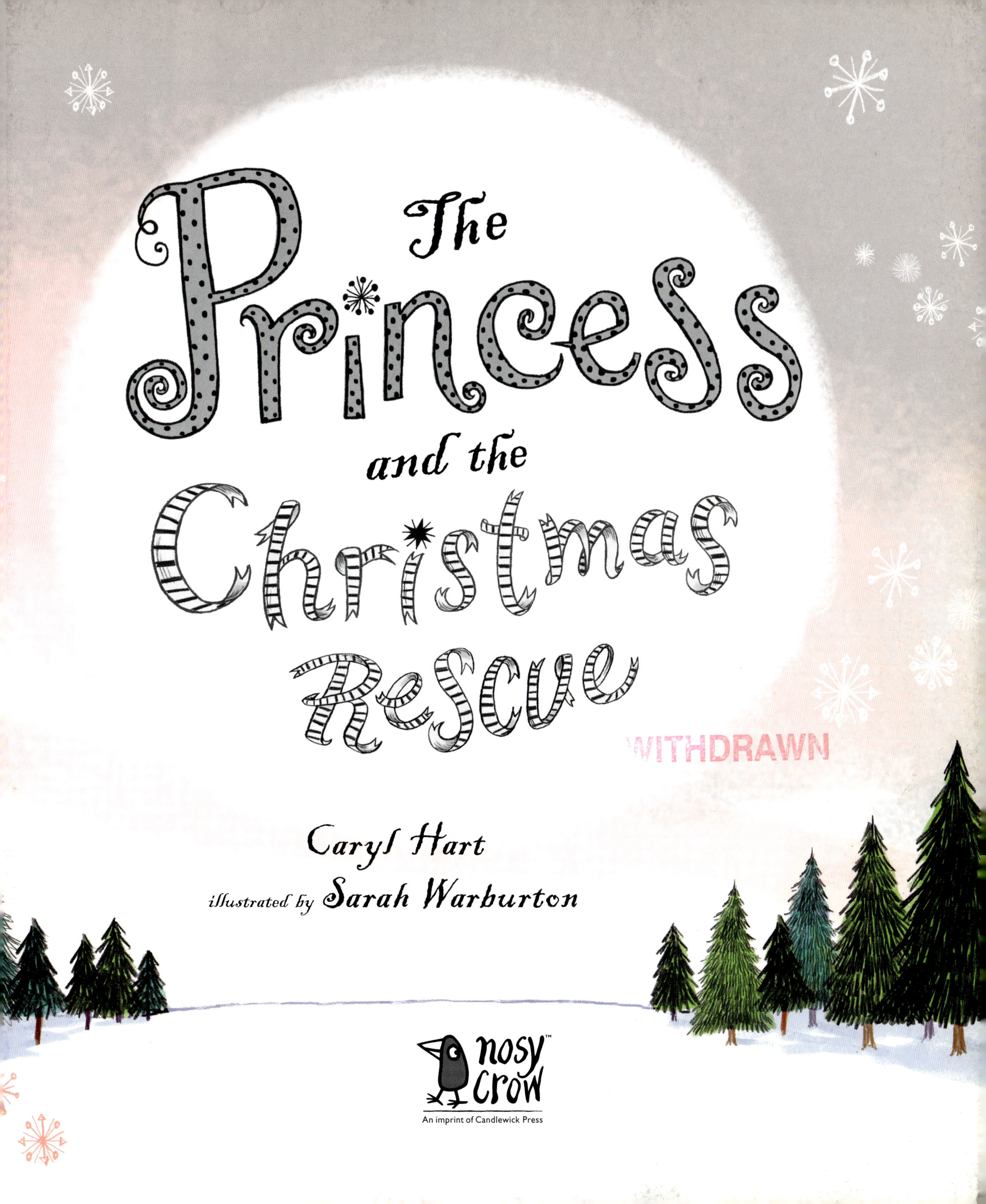

The Princess and the Christmas Rescue

Caryl Hart

illustrated by Sarah Warburton

nosy crow™
An imprint of Candlewick Press

On top of the world where the icy winds blow,
a beautiful palace grows out of the snow.
It sits in a forest of towering trees.
The snow is so deep it goes up past your knees.

The place was just perfect for children to play,
yet the princess who lived there stayed *inside* all day.
The king said, "That forest is scary and wild,
with tigers and bears that could eat a small child."

Now, Princess Eliza was brainy and bright.
She kept herself busy from morning till night.
With wood, lots of string, and some pieces of wire,
the princess could make anything you'd desire.

ODD-
SOCK
SORTER

The king said, “This hobby is far from princess-y.
Your dress gets so dusty. Your room is so messy.”
“It’s great that you make all these things,” the queen said.
“But how about making a friend now instead?”

But how? thought Eliza. *I really don't know.*
Perhaps I could bake one from gingerbread dough.
But when he was cooked, the boy hopped off the tray,
then stuck out his tongue and . . .

SKEDADDLED away!

Eliza sighed. "I'm getting nowhere like this."
She found a large frog and she gave him a kiss.
She hoped he'd turn into a prince before long.
The frog just said, "Croak," and then . . .

BOING, he was gone!

"Oh, well," said Eliza. "I've braided my hair.
I'll dangle it out of that window up there.
A knight might climb up — we could play a fun game."
She waited for hours . . . but nobody came.

Poor Princess Eliza looked over the trees
and sniffed at some smoke blowing in on the breeze.
"A frog's not a friend, I can't make one from dough,
and nobody visits because of the snow.

Perhaps there is someone out there I can ask
to help me succeed at this difficult task.
I won't be gone long and I'll wear this warm cloak.
I'll visit whoever is making that smoke."

The princess set off through the glittering frost.
The woods were confusing and soon she was lost.
A huge shaggy shape loomed up out of the snow.
"The tigers and bears," gulped Eliza. "Oh, no!"

"Oh, please don't be frightened," a gentle voice said,
and there stood a reindeer with bells on its head.
"I'll take you to safety — just climb on my back.
We'll go to the house at the end of this track."

Eliza crept in through the open front door,
past huge sacks of letters piled up on the floor,
and there in a room filled with untidy shelves
sat a miserable bunch of forlorn-looking elves.

There was Bertie and Gertie and Felix and Fred,
and Pixie and Dixie and Nora and Ned.
The biggest was Gordon, the smallest was Nell.
Each elf wore a pointy hat topped with a bell.

"Hello?" said Eliza. "I've got a quick question.
How can I make friends? Might you have a suggestion?"
"We're sorry," said Felix. "Our boss has the flu.
We'd all love to chat — but there's TOO much to do."

"We must read these letters and sort all these toys
to wrap up and give out to good girls and boys."
"I'll help," said Eliza. "I really don't mind."
"There's no point," said Bertie. "We're too far behind."

But Princess Eliza knew just what to do:
When the elves went to bed,
she found scissors and glue.

With paper clips, sticky tape,
cardboard, and string,
she made a cool gadgety
speed-reading thing.

Next morning, the elves found a long list of names
that matched every child with the right toys and games.
"Amazing!" cheered Felix and Fred in delight.
"Somebody read all those letters last night!"

The elves and Eliza worked hard, side by side.
"This Christmas list goes on *forever!*" Nell cried.
"We'll never get finished before Christmas Day!"
"There, there," said Eliza. "I'm sure there's a way."

That night, young Eliza sprang back into action.
She made a robotic gift-picking contraption.
She flicked the big switch, and in no time at all,
it had all the presents lined up in the hall.

"Bazonkers!" cried Pixie and Dixie next morning.
The elves were so sleepy, they couldn't stop yawning.
"Look! SOMEONE has sorted the toys in the night.
We've checked the list twice, and they've done it just right!"

LARGE
MEDIUM
SMALL

Then Nora found sticky tape, paper, and bows,
but wrapping is tricky, as everyone knows.

The elves and Eliza were doing quite well
till Ned cried, "Gadzookers!
We've lost little Nell!"

By bedtime, they'd run out of paper and glue.
"Oh, Princess," said Gordon.
"What *are* we to do?"

"Don't worry," Eliza said, rubbing her eyes.
"Perhaps in the morning you'll get a surprise."

And there the next morning, all sparkling and clean,
they found a neat wind-up gift-wrapping machine.
It gave a loud whirr, then a clunk and a hum,
and wrapped all the presents and labeled each one.

"Ho ho!" boomed a voice. "Well, I rather like that!"
And there stood a man in a red coat and hat.
"Oh, SANTA! You're better!" the happy elves cried.
"Your sleigh is all ready—it's waiting outside!"

"A kind person helped us, but no one knows who."
"Princess," asked Santa, "could it have been YOU?"
Eliza blushed. "Yes, but don't tell my mom, please.
She said I should stop making gadgets like these."

"What nonsense!" said Santa. "I'll give her a call.
You've been clever and generous. Not naughty at all!
Now, come with us all on a magical flight
and help us deliver the presents tonight."

The sleigh traveled fast across countries and nations,
all thanks to Eliza's quick modifications.
"We've done it!" beamed Santa. "And super quick, too!
But now it's your turn. What can WE do for YOU?"

"There's one thing," Eliza said, blushing bright pink.
"I need a new friend. Could you help, do you think?"
"Oh, Princess," said Santa. "I think you will find
you've made LOTS of friends just by being so kind."

The queen heard the news of her daughter's good deeds
and said to the king, "I know what our child needs."
They sold a few paintings, some clothes, and some jewels
and built her a workshop with all the best tools.

ELIZA

The princess invented a snow-powered sleigh
and played in the woods with the elves every day.
She helped out each Christmas with kindness and skill,
and as far as I know, she is doing it still!

THE END!